BEFORE HER

GRACE PARKES

1

Working behind a bar for almost 5 years had taken the joy out of customer service for Cara Taylor. How many times can you listen to the same conversation, about the same ex-wife whilst you serve the same beer to the same drunk, creepy guy?

Nothing exciting happens in Elverford – at least it hadn't for the twenty five years of her life.

∼

'Do you think I'll be working at the Oak forever?' Cara said as she rolled her eyes and spun her bottle of beer around her hand, slowly peeling off the label.

'Depends. Can you be bothered to leave Elverford? Not many people seem to. The Oak is a pretty good job, low stress, and you get more than minimum wage.' Jenny smiled at Cara, reminding her of the reality of the village they had grown up in. You either escape it or you die there.

'At least I live with you now. Twenty-five and living with my mother. Jeez, that's enough to drive anyone crazy. Also, what do you mean *low stress?* You try and listen to Stewart harp on about his sexless relationship with his poor wife for days on end.' Cara raised her eyebrows and took a swig of her tatty bottle of beer.

'You are right, and you are so welcome! It's nice to have the company. Especially after Michelle left.' As Jenny looked out of the window Cara could see that Michelle was still a sore subject.

Jenny and Michelle met years in the village. Michelle had moved there to start a gardening and landscaping business. It didn't take long until Jenny spotted her bronze, muscular body, bending over decking and turning poky patches of grass into something beautiful. Three months ago, she spotted Michelle's same toned body bending over another woman in their bed.

'Well, I'm glad to be here. Have you heard much from Michelle?' Cara felt like Jenny needed to talk more, she hadn't processed any of it.

'Not really. I see her posts on Facebook looking all fucking happy go lucky with Sue. I mean, *Sue- of all people*? What has Sue got that I *haven't*?' Jenny raised her hands bitterly in the air, genuinely concerned that boring Sue, who was ten years older than her and rough around the edges, had managed to ruin her deepest love.

'Maybe Michelle just wasn't happy? I don't know. It doesn't take away the fact that it was totally wrong, and she should've communicated with her words rather than her fingers. I always thought there was something odd about her,' Cara replied as she shrugged her shoulders.

'Ouch! It's only been a few months mate. Then again, who knows how long it could've gone on for if I hadn't caught them red-handed. I bet there are loads of secret lesbians around here.' Jenny raised her eyebrows and finished her beer. Sue wasn't always a lesbian; in fact, she had been married to a local farmer but only out of *tradition*. Michelle had opened her eyes to the world she never knew she craved. 'Have you heard much from Amy?'

Amy was Cara's last relationship, and only serious girlfriend. They spent two long years together but Cara knew it wouldn't last from the moment it started. All Cara wanted was someone who could make her smile and someone who would give back at least a little of the love she had to give. As a true cancerian, wearing her heart on her sleeve, Amy managed to trample all over it. Looking back, Cara had no idea how she put up with it all for so long. The relentless arguing, the simple incompatibilities, the broken trust. All of it was a concoction for disaster. The final straw was Amy proposing, making Cara imagine what dreary future would lay ahead. Subsequently she declined and broke off the relationship and spent the weekend celebrating with Jenny over bottles of wine and takeaway. Ever since Amy, Cara vowed to never let anyone take over her life again. To never let anyone, waste her time.

Cara smirked and took a drink of her beer before answering. 'Nah. I get the odd text but I don't reply. I can't even be civil with her because she manages to start an argument.'

'You dodged a bullet there, mate.' Jenny laughed.

'More like I escaped a future of hell!'

Jenny and Cara grew up together in the picturesque village of Elverford. They went to the same school, the same parties, and were part of the same small circle of people their age in the village. After leaving college neither of them had left the village, they had already become part of its bones. Part of the tatty wall that kids grew up sitting on adjacent from the church. The essence of the village community – or something like that. Elverford had a spell on the people who resided there. They didn't often leave. It might be the beautiful, rural location set near the peak district, or that it was like the land that time forgot. People forgot that there was more out there, either that or they refused to acknowledge it.

'I think I'll move out of here… one day. I said that before though and then I ended up buying another property! So, let's face it, I probably won't.' Jenny bought a property after inheriting money from her father's death. At twenty-six years old she had two houses in the village, one of which she now shared with Cara.

'Thank god you do though. I would've exploded if I had to spend another year with Mira.' Cara opened two more beers, handing one to Jenny.

'Oh, come on she's not that bad! All mums are annoying, aren't they? Mine's fucking crazy!' Jenny laughed, sweeping her bright ginger hair over her left shoulder.

'Come on. You've known her all of your life too. She's a nightmare!' Cara rolled her eyes. Mira was a nightmare mum. She was overly involved. She loved to hoard rubbish, and frequently seduce married men. Unfortunately, Cara didn't know her biological father, she was the result of another illicit affair back in 1994. However, she was almost certain she could be the actual milk man's daughter. Her deep blue eyes and olive skin complexion resembled his a little too much.

'True. She's a character that's for sure. I do love her though,' Jenny said as she scrunched up her pointy nose and smiled, showing her slightly nicotine dampened teeth.

'So, what's going on with Elmore Street?' Cara liked to know what Jenny was up to with her property. Elmore street was where Jenny's two-bed semi-detached home that had been empty for a while due to previous nightmare tenants doing a runner and trashing the house.

'I was reluctant to rent it out after that pair of wankers; however, I think I have someone interested! She's coming over soon I hope, to have a look around.' Jenny supped her beer and reached for her cigarettes. 'Want one?'

'No thanks. You know I have to be at least 6/10 stressed or drunk to consider smoking. Also, that'll be good. Extra income for you and maybe some new life in the village!' Cara was desperate for new faces. The local town didn't have much to offer either.

'Yes, a new face would be refreshing. Maybe you need to meet someone new? You need some fire in your pants. Why don't you get on Tinder? I'm on it. I love it. I've got 3 matches.' Jenny laughed, fully aware that she took an awful picture and was awful at talking to people online.

'Ah, all the good-looking women live miles away. There's no talent in Elverford *apart from us* – of course.' Cara grinned and broke into laughter. Her teeth were naturally perfect. No braces, no dental work, just nice white perfect teeth. As she laughed her wavy blonde hair bobbed over her shoulders, resembling a stereotypical Cornwall surfer girl.

Jenny winked and raised her bottle in the air. 'To the best lesbians in this shitty village!' They clinked glasses and laughed to themselves, so blissfully unaware of how things could change.

2

The shower was at maximum temperature. Cara loved the feeling of the beating hot water against her skin. She lathered herself in moisturising shower cream and made an effort to relax. Her skin was soft as she ran her hands down her sides. Her curves were beautifully placed. An hourglass figure. As the soap suds ran away from her skin, she reached to the shampoo and conditioner in an attempt to revitalise her blonde locks which she never gave much time for. Working in a pub meant scraping the hair tight and up, away from the face.

The shower was Cara's favourite place to think. The hot water rinsed her olive skin clean. She took a deep breath, ran her hands over her face and was ready to go and get ready for work.

Another shift at the pub, locking up in the early hours of the morning. Turfing out the local alcoholics. The same thing every week. Cara had no idea why these men wanted to spend their lives in the pub. She had no idea why their wives put up with them. All she knew is she was saving her money and wanted to get out of there one day, one way or another.

Maybe this wasn't the right time to find someone new to focus on? Her thoughts overtook.

She stepped out of the shower and wrapped herself up in a big grey bath towel as she heard Jenny fussing around outside of her room.

'Is everything alright out there?'

'Yeah, I'm looking for my leather jacket. Do you have it?' Jenny hadn't been fitting into her usual attire due to eating her feelings after the breakup, however, after recently joining the local weight watchers' group she had shifted a stone and had received *Slimmer of the Week* award.

'Why, where you off at this late hour? No sorry, not in here!' Cara walked over and opened her bedroom door.

'I have a date. I told you I was on Tinder, didn't I? Well, I'm meeting Kirsty tonight.' Jenny grinned.

'*Putting on your red light*?' Cara couldn't help herself.

'Oh, stop it! She lives in town, we're meeting at Grand Central for a drink. I'm fucking nervous. I haven't been on a date in like years. She looks hot though, and like she could throw me around the bedroom. She also plays rugby and you know I like those big muscly rugby girls.'

Jenny was clearly excited as her eyes lit up just at the thought of watching a woman in a scrum.

'Wow! I hope it goes well. Make sure you text me, okay? Traffic light system. Green for *yes it's great*, Amber for *oh god I'm not sure* and Red for *get me the fuck out of here*. Here, I've got a jacket you can try on.' Cara walked over to her wardrobe and began to shuffle through her hangers. 'Here you go! One leather jacket.'

'You're a size 12 and I'm about 16 now, so I doubt I'll get it on, also no offence but my tits are way bigger than yours.' Jenny had little confidence in herself.

'Oh, just try it on! It's spacious.' Cara threw it at her.

Jenny got the jacket on and took a long hard look at herself in the mirror. 'You know what, I look fucking great!'

'You sure do. Also, you should let your hair down. I love your ginger curls.' Cara put her hand on her hip, keeping her towel to her body with the other hand.

'Thanks, babe. You're the best. I'm not hugging you though because you're basically naked. Have a good shift and I'll text you later,' Jenny said as she made her way out of Cara's room to wait for her taxi.

'Good luck! You look great. Remember, don't panic. You're weird when you panic.' Cara shouted.

'Point noted,' Jenny shouted before shutting the door behind her to get into the taxi.

3

The Oak was a small pub, with not much room behind the bar, mainly due to the landlords obsession with flavoured Gins. The back wall was littered with shelves and an array of gins from all over the place. The décor questionable, like an old farm house. The Oak did have charm though, and the locals loved it.

Cara was in charge of the bar with two young waitresses primarily taking orders and running the food in and out of the kitchen. They were like small robots with ponytails, wandering around with note pads and a smile of their little teen faces. Her manager Dan, who couldn't be anymore creepy or arrogant if he tried, strolled around chatting to the customers, then would disappear for hours on end. Cara could run the bar with her eyes shut so she didn't mind being on her own, plus the locals loved her.

She could pour the best pint in the village.

'One more of the same please, sweetheart.' Eric handed over his change. He didn't need to let her know what he was drinking. Cara had served him the same lager for five years now.

'No problem!' Cara grabbed the glass and started pouring the pint, noticing in her peripheral vision that Dan had decided to turn up. He entered the pub and shook hands with all punters. He knew they kept his pockets heavy and that he had the charm to keep them there.

'Good evening Cara. You're looking just as delicious as ever.' Dan brushed pass Cara and reached over to the till to take out some cash.

Cara cringed. Dan was cringeworthy.

'Thanks'. Cara replied in a monotone voice.

'I see you've got that tight top on again! *Tits sell beer.*' Dan laughed as his fat fingers grabbed the cash out of the till. She was sure he wasn't paying tax on half of it.

'How many times do I have to tell you that my tits are nothing to do with you?' The regular vulgar comments had gone past a joke and almost verged into harassment.

Dan held his hands up in the air and turned on his larger-than-life smile. 'Okay, I apologise. It's just a joke, Cara. You know, something funny. You're touchy today.' Dan rolled his eyes at Eric and continued rummaging through cash.

Cara rolled her eyes at Eric too, as he saw how difficult Dan could be.

He only took over the pub a year ago and he was great at creeping out women.

'Thanks, lovely.' Eric took his pint and sipped it slowly, leaving a white foamy moustache on his old wrinkly upper lip.

Dan smiled at them both as she made his way towards the door. 'You're locking up tonight Cara, I've got to go and pick my daughter up.' He winked as he ruffled his hands through his died black hair which resembled something from the film Grease.

'Sure thing.' Cara knew she would be anyway, and she also knew Dan wouldn't be picking his daughter up. More like he would be picking women up, luring them in with cash and charm.

Dan said his goodbyes on the way out of the pub. The door closed behind him and Eric looked at Cara as he raised his eyebrows. 'Ignore him. We all know he's a wanker. It was much better when Keith was running the gaff.'

'It was better then, but if he was still here, he would probably be... dead!' It sounded dramatic but the problem with Keith was that he liked to drink the profits.

'True point. At least you're here, and for the record, I don't care about your tits. I like your... personality.' Eric smiled and sipped his pint.

He was one of Cara's favourite customers.

'Thanks, Eric. You know how to make a girl feel special.' Cara smiled.

'I've had decades of practice sweetheart. Always remember you must live your life.' Even though Eric had a smile on his face, there was a deep sadness behind his sunken grey eyes.

He had confessed to Cara late one night that he never really loved his wife, Marianne. He was in love with her brother, Michael. Michael was married to Sue, but also had a deep love for Eric. Nobody would say anything, and they hid it all of their lives, until Michael passed away and left a note for his wife explaining why he had left certain sentimental items to Eric in his will.

As men of the older generations in a small farming village, coming out would never be easy, especially in the land that time forgot.

Eric kept his secret to himself, even though it destroyed him.

4

Jenny had spent the night at Kirsty's house in the local town after a seemingly successful first date. She never texted Cara with the traffic light system as she lost herself in Kirsty and her muscular physique. It was midday and Jenny was sprawled across their corner sofa with a cold flannel on her head and a litre bottle of water by her side.

'Good night then?' Cara walked in with a brew and sat on the other end of the sofa, stretching out her legs across the blankets.

'Oh, my days. So good. I haven't had an orgasm like that in... forever.' Jenny pressed the flannel to her head as a smile crept across her face.

'Wow! So much for not fucking on the first date?' Cara laughed as she enjoyed her coffee, it was always essential she had her morning/afternoon coffee after a late-night locking up at the pub. Even when you get home from bar work, it's hard to wind down. Cara found herself lying in bed until 4 am mindlessly scrolling through her social media feeds.

'I don't care. She charmed the pants off of me. I'm all for doing what you want, when you want, how you want. If you're both available. Sexual liberation. She actually managed to pick me up and throw me around.' Jenny managed to stretch out her arm to reach her water.

'Good for you! I'm all for it! That's

what you get for dating a rugby girl. Will you be seeing each other again?' Cara grabbed the blanket and wrapped herself up.

'Yes. Tonight actually. She's coming over here, do you mind?' With one eye open Jenny peered down the sofa at Cara to gain her consent.

'Of course, I don't mind. Do you need me out of the way?' Cara replied as she comforted Jenny's leg.

'No way, this is your home too. I'll try and keep the noise down though.' Jenny laughed.

'I might go out. I can't cope with your sex noises.' Cara's hand rested on her head as she shook it.

'Ah come on, don't be like that. You're just jealous. I'm telling you, get on tinder. You won't meet anyone in that stinking old pub you know.'

'You are right, but I've been thinking, I don't want to lose my focus. I'm saving up money and want to travel or move somewhere new eventually. I don't want to be here forever.' Cara smiled at Jenny, knowing that she was a friend who would always be there.

'Good for you, but you can have sex, great sex, without all of the emotions.' Jenny pushed herself into a seated position as she gulped down her water.

'Really? In what lesbian planet does that exist?' Cara laughed.

'*Very funny*. Mm, I think your mum just walked past the window.' Jenny caught sight of Mira.

You could spot her a mile off with her dyed jet-black hair.

'Ah great.' Cara sighed as Mira banged on the door.

'Come in!' Jenny shouted, luckily the living room was right by the hallway so if you shouted loud enough you didn't have to move.

Mira made her way into the house;

you could hear her before you saw her. Her bangles and dangly earrings as gothic and audible as ever.

'Afternoon girls. My gosh, what are you doing lazing around on this beautiful day? I've brought you a red velvet cake.' Mira smiled and rummaged into her bright coloured canvas bag which had the face of a pug printed on it.

'What are you after? I know cake means you want something.' Cara wasn't stupid. She knew her mum too well.

'I made you it out of love. However, I do have a favour to ask. It's unrelated to the cake. The thing is I saw Jim last night and his wife spotted him walking away from the house. So.. I just need an alibi that you were there? He said that he is going to leave Joan for me, it's just a matter of time – before you get all judge-mental Cara Malara.' Mira was in her own world.

Cara felt her blood boiling as she held

her anger internally. 'You need to stop fucking with married men mum. You always get hurt, and so do their wives.'

'What do you mean? It's not like there's been many...' Mira was defensive about the truth.

'I'm not getting into it mum, but I will not give you an alibi. I'm not getting involved in this again. You get me into shit!' Cara looked away, disengaging from eye contact.

Jenny sunk into the sofa and cringed.

'Well I'll tell her you were there and if she asks you, then fine, say what you will. You're such a misery! It's not my fault that his wife won't make him happy.' Mira swung her hair over her shoulder and made her way out of the house.

Cara took a deep breath and stared at Jenny. 'Wow. I can't cope with that woman. She's the one who needs Tinder.'

'I think she has an obsession with

married men. It's weird. Maybe she needs to be a unicorn?' Jenny laughed.

'What on earth do you mean, *a unicorn*?' Cara scrunched up her button nose.

'A single woman who meets up with other couples. Although your mum doesn't strike me as gay in any way.' Jenny looked up, imagining far too much for her own good.

'Oh hell, no. She only just copes with me being a lesbian.' Cara unscrunched her face and finished her brew. 'Anyway, I can't think about this anymore. What is your plan for tonight?'

'I'm cooking! Don't laugh.' It was a clear fact that Jenny was terrible at cooking.

'Please, just order a takeaway. Remember that lasagne you made that somehow turned into a meatloaf?' It was a running joke that Jenny should not be near a kitchen.

'Yes, I do. Maybe I could take her to the Oak. I like the meals in there. I might even get a discount.' Jenny said as she finished off her water which was slowing hydrating her back to life.

'Good idea! I might see if they need any extra hands there tonight. I'm looking forward to meeting Kirsty... although is it a bit much you going to the pub for a meal on your second date?'

Jenny thought about it for a moment, 'Maybe, but I don't care. I don't want to waste time so it either works or it doesn't. Either way, the sex was incredible.'

'Fair point!' Cara laughed.

'Right, I need to peel myself off of this sofa and shower away last night.' Jenny smiled.

'Ew. Make sure you clean the shower afterward. I don't want your morning after water.' Cara shuddered and made the most of the extra room on the sofa.

'Sure thing!' As Jenny stood up her

knees cracked, and she stooped over like an old woman. 'I need to stretch more, or maybe I stretched the wrong way last night.'

'Too much info! Bye!' Cara grinned and reached for the remote to watch some mind-numbing television. Mira knew how to get under her skin.

Jenny popped her head around the door before going upstairs to sort her life out, 'Oh I do have a favour to ask actually... all being well, Kirsty and I are going for a mucky night away at a hotel on Saturday, but I have the new tenant arriving at Elmore. Can you meet her there at 12 and hand over the keys and paperwork? She sounded nice on the phone.'

'Yeah sure. Surprisingly I'm not working until 7 pm on Saturday. It will be the first Saturday in months where I have seen what the outside world looks like for the majority of the day.' Cara sighed, still flicking through channels.

'Perfect. You're the best!' Jenny dragged herself up the stairs ready to spruce up for her evening with Kirsty.

As Cara sunk into the deep sofa, she felt her eyes become heavier. It wasn't long until she had drifted into a midday snooze.

5

Later that day, the clock struck 7 pm and Kirsty was due to arrive. Jenny made her way into the kitchen to pour herself a gin and tonic and get another glimpse of herself in the mirror.

'Do I look hot? Be honest.'

'You're *smoking* hot. I'm so excited to meet her.' Cara was desperate for some excitement.

'Oh my god, was that the door? I'll go and check.' Jenny rushed over pulling down her tight red dress, so it was perfectly in place and not riding up her arse or tits. She opened the door and let out a squeal. 'Come in, come and meet my housemate and oldest friend Cara!'

Kirsty was tall, with dark black hair tied up in a ponytail. She had muscular shoulders and deep brown eyes. You could tell she would win a tackle with her eyes closed. She looked sporty and strong. It was evident her body was in great shape through her skin-tight black jeans and maroon top. It made a good match with Jenny's dress and hair.

'Hey! Nice to meet you. I've already heard so much about you.' Kirsty held out her hand to Cara, who immediately noticed the size of her palms and fingers. She tried her best not to make any sarcastic remarks.

'Hello! Welcome to our humble abode. It's so good to meet you too.' Cara held out her hand as Kirsty firmly shook it.

'What would you like to drink? I've got everything!' Jenny was eager to please.

'How about beer? Any will do.' Kirsty had a warming smile and Cara could see why Jenny already liked her so much. 'So, Cara, I hear you're Elverford's best barmaid. We're heading to the pub tonight for food apparently, will you be joining us?'

'I wouldn't want to be the third wheel! You two have a nice meal together, enjoy yourselves.' Cara knew it would cramp Jenny's over keen style.

'No, honestly you should join us. I'd

like to get to know you better. You don't mind do you, babe?' Kirsty called through to the kitchen.

'Not at all, honey.' Cara knew Jenny would be slightly pissed off, but she would get over it.

Cara tucked her wavy blonde curls behind her ear and thought about how nice it would be to just enjoy a drink and a meal without serving it to shitty customers. 'Okay, then I'll join you! They do great burgers.'

'Awesome.' Kirsty smiled as Jenny trotted over passing her a bottle of beer. 'Thanks, beautiful.' Kirsty planted a kiss on Jenny's lips which made her instantly blush.

The three of them went into the kitchen as Jenny opened the back door to light a cigarette. Cara could see Kirsty's face change. 'I guess you're not a smoker then?' Cara asked Kirsty as she pulled herself up onto the countertop.

'Nah, I used to, then I quit! I hated wheezing in the morning or going outside in the cold. Plus playing rugby and smoking wasn't a great combination. You should quit, Jenny. It's a terrible habit,' Kirsty said still with a smile on her face.

'I know. I will one day. Before I'm thirty. They say it's good to quit before you hit thirty.' Jenny loved smoking.

'And may I ask who *they* are?' Cara sarcastically replied.

'*Har har* very funny.' Jenny puffed away on her cig.

'So, Cara, are you seeing anyone?'

Kirsty was keen to make a good impression with Jenny's best friend.

She was already doing much better than Jenny's ex Michelle. She was a cold-hearted bitch at times.

'Nope. I split up with my ex about a year ago and I've just been taking some time to look after myself you know? I can't be arsed with drama.' Cara rolled her eyes.

'Well funnily, I live with my best friend who is also a lesbian, and she is also single. I was thinking maybe you should meet her?'

'Blimey. I've only known you 15 minutes and you're hooking me up with single lesbians. I like you already!' Cara laughed and smiled at Jenny.

'I don't fuck around!' Kirsty smiled. Cara knew she wasn't joking as she was already in Jenny's house on the second date. 'She's not dramatic either...'

'Are you sure? Because they all say that, and then they are.' Cara had had enough of dramatic.
'I promise.'

Jenny closed the door and popped a tic tac into her mouth in the hope it would take away her cigarette tainted breath. 'Let's just start by going for a meal together and enjoying our night. I can't let Cara get swept away by any more crazy women. She's in a good place. Aren't you hun?'

Cara looked up and took a moment to think about that. Was she in a good place? She had no idea. She was just plodding along in her life. The same old every day. Cara knew something would come up eventually, but she had no idea what it would be... yet.

'I know what I am. I'm hungry. Let's finish this and go!?'

'Good idea. I'm ready for a burger.' Kirsty put her bottle in the glass bin and smiled at Jenny.

They made their way to the pub and spent the evening drinking, laughing, and eating. Cara found it refreshing to be on the other side of the bar and to see Jenny look genuinely happy for the first time in ages. She started to miss feeling happy. She missed how good someone could make you feel. Sometimes the bad parts of a relationship seep into your soul and turn you into a negative emotion blocker. Cara knew she was ready to find her heart again.

6

The bleak weather of April began settling into the breezy Saturday air. The sunshine didn't know if it had the energy to fight for its appearance as the clouds clogged up the sky. Cara had the house to herself as Jenny had just left to go away for the night at a rural hotel with Kirsty. She had left her a pile of things to take over to the house on Elmore Street to drop off for the new tenant, Frankie.

Cara imagined how much she would

love to have her own property that she could do up and rent out. She loved making places homely. Growing up with Mira made that impossible as she was a prolific hoarder and a hater of housework. Losing herself in these daydreams had become more frequent along with the want to escape from the boredom surrounding her. A change was needed.

Cara put on her black Chelsea boots and made her way out into the cool air wrapped up in a thick fleeced coat. On her way out of the house, she glanced at herself in the mirror and admired her eye makeup. Sometimes a little makeup made her feel sassy.

Elmore Street was less than a 10-minute walk and she loved the fresh air. The smell of damp grass. The trees gracefully swaying in the wind.

As she walked down the streets she grew up on, the nostalgia hit her in the chest. The happy memories of playing on the streets with her friends. The sweet, naivety of childhood, where responsibilities did not come into play. Those sweet days where you just need to remember to be in by 6 for dinner. You carry around a little change for the ice cream van. The walk flashed by in countless memories and Cara had reached Elmore Street. Cara squinted over to the house as she noticed an unfamiliar person unloading boxes out of a bright blue pick-up truck. She knew it must be Frankie. She also thought she looked hot, even from the distance. Cara approached the back of the car and attempted to get her attention, so she didn't take her by surprise as she was bending over into the back of her truck. She noticed her sun-kissed skin and strong shoulders showing as she was bending over grabbing a box, exposing the tattoo on the bottom of back that she couldn't quite make out.

Cara knew she was tough to be wearing anything less than a coat in this weather.

'Hi! Are you Frankie? I'm Jenny's friend and housemate. I have some things for you!' Cara smiled with a warmth that could energise the cold air.

Frankie turned around as she held the big box close to her chest. She was at least 3 inches taller than Cara and had deep, dark eyes that already looked like they were haunted by a thousand sad stories. She smiled, highlighting the creases at the side of her eyes. 'Hey. Nice to meet you, sorry I didn't get your name?'

'I'm Cara Taylor. I've got some paperwork for you and the spare key. Jenny is away for the night, so I said I'd stop by, see how you're getting on and if you need a hand at all.' Cara was still smiling. Frankie was beautiful. She noticed her rough looking hands gripping on to the box, they looked like hard working hands.

'Ah great. Nice to meet you Miss Taylor. Do you mind just following me in? Kind of got my hands full already.' Frankie didn't sound local either. Her accent sounding slightly Scottish.

'Yes, sure. Do you need some help?' Cara didn't have much muscle, but she noticed plenty of little things loose in the back of the truck. Including the kettle, tea bags, and milk. Frankie had made a special stop on the way to grab the essentials.

'Oh please. Can you grab the drinking supplies?' Frankie smiled, nodded towards Cara, and made her way inside. The box in her hands looked heavy but the weight off it didn't seem to bother Frankie.

Cara couldn't help but find her eyes looking ahead as she walked into the house. Frankie's tall physique, her tanned skin, her ragged jeans, and a tight tank top exposing her defined shoulders. Her dark brown hair was up in a tight bun. Cara felt a little spark in her core.

Who on earth is Frankie and which lesbian goddess dropped her off here?

That was one of her many fleeting thoughts dazzling her mind.

After grabbing the drinking necessities, Cara managed to carry it all inside along with the paperwork from Jenny. Frankie had dumped the boxes in the middle of the living room.

'Thank god this place is partially furnished! I'd be sleeping on the carpet if not. I didn't come with much other than the essentials. My apologies for looking so rough – I'm not usually like that... well sometimes.'

'Oh really? Where did you come from? You look fine to me.' Cara was instantly intrigued. She liked the rugged look. A flickering image of her being thrown around by Frankie swept through her mind. She tried not to physically shake her head attempting to get the thought away from her brain.

Frankie sighed and grabbed the kettle from Cara. 'A friend's house. I've been renting a room for a while. Can I get you a drink? I have tea, water, or... coffee.' Frankie made her way to the kitchen, filled up the kettle, and retrieved the mugs and spoon out of the box labelled *Kitchen Shit*.

'I'll have a tea please. Just milk, no sugar.' Cara perched on the armchair, admiring Frankie's back from behind.

'Sure thing. So how do you know Jenny? She sounds nice, we've spoken on the phone. She seems like a great landlady. I'm a pretty easy-going tenant. Keep myself to myself. Does she like dogs? I've been thinking of rescuing one.' Frankie was eager to make a coffee.

It had been a long day and she wasn't interested in divulging about herself.

'We grew up together and then after I got completely fed up living with my crazy mother, she broke up with her ex-girlfriend and I moved in! She absolutely loves dogs, actually.' Cara wasn't sure if she was oversharing or if it was fine to be that open with her best friend's new tenant who she only just met.

'Ex-girlfriend? I thought I'd be the *only gay in this village.*' Frankie laughed as she poured the boiled water into her favourite set of mugs with motivational quotes on. It's the little things in life.

'You'd be surprised. Elverford is a strange place.'

'Strange? Is that what you think of us lesbians?' As Frankie walked in, she had a smile perched across her defined features. Cara noticed the piercing on her lip catching the light.

'I didn't mean it like that! I'm actually one of those *village lesbians*.' Cara winked and took the brew off of Frankie. She looked at the mug that said *c'est la vie* and smiled. She liked Frankie already.

'Really? Well, can I join your gang?' Frankie's eye lit up as she sat down on the opposite sofa. It was evident that there was something brewing in the air, other than the coffee.

'You sure can! Anyway, here's the paperwork. I can't get distracted with all this lesbian talk. Have you checked out the local amenities yet? We've got a shop, a pub – which I work at may I add – and a hairdresser. We also have a great Chinese. Are you familiar with the area?' Cara found the lesbian chat was making her slightly heated. She didn't know why. It seemed safer to change the subject.

An unexpected nervousness took over her and she found that too many words were coming out at once.

'Wow. Everything you need in one place. I used to live in Charlton so I'm fairly familiar with it.' Frankie smiled and sipped her coffee. Charlton was the local town; however, the gay scene was so small Cara found it hard to believe she had never seen Frankie before.

She knew she would remember if she had.

'Ah, nice. What on earth brings you to the land that time forgot?'

'I wanted a change. Somewhere more rural. I have my own business. I guess you could call me a handywoman. Moving out here would hopefully mean more projects to work with there being so much land and property.'

'Ooo a handywoman? You're good

with a power tool?' Cara laughed, tucking her blonde waves behind her ear.

'I sure am! If you need a hole drilling, let me know.' Frankie winked as Cara felt a rush of heat flood her body as she almost spat out her tea.

'*What an offer*. Anyway, I have work tonight at The Oak, so I best be getting off. If there is anything you need, I have written down my number on the bottom of that file.' Cara smiled aware her cheeks were bright red, she needed to get out there before she jumped on Jenny's new tenant.

'Sure thing. Thanks, Cara. I might pop down the pub later and check out the local talent.' Frankie laughed and stood up to see Cara out.

'Enjoy unpacking. Maybe I'll see you later!' Cara smiled as she stood up and began to make her way out.

'See you later.' Frankie closed the

door and Cara made her way down the gravel path.

Cara felt flushed in her cheeks. She made her way back home walking as brisk as she could to race off her extra adrenaline. Who the fuck is Frankie? Cara wanted to know more.

7

Frankie finished her coffee and watched Cara walk down the driveway. She noticed how her she walked in such a graceful manner. How her blonde hair bobbed by her side with the motion of her steps. She liked the bright colour of neon pink on her fingernails. Something was warming about Cara.

Looking down at the boxes in the living room began to feel overwhelming. The old boxes of memories that she tried to forget at times. Frankie decided to make a start. The first box had a case inside with photographs. She opened up the packet and grabbed out the printed photos. Actual photographs definitely felt like a thing of the past. She looked down and smiled at pictures of her and her mother. Happily playing in the sand. Looking at her mother now was almost like looking in a mirror. Time had passed by. So much time. So much had happened in 5 years. It was almost too much to comprehend. The next photo was of her and her pets. Growing up on a farm in Scotland allowed room for extra animals, even if some weren't meant to be pets.

The best thing about the farm was the animals, and the freedom. All of the space to roam. Nobody to bother young Frankie who was quite happy getting dirty playing in the fields and farm yards. *Such a little lesbian* Frankie thought to herself admiring the little dungarees she was wearing.

Frankie felt a flutter in her heart and put the photos aside. Her heartbeat began to quicken. She took a deep breath and controlled her breathing. The joyous anxiety was back. Luckily Frankie was a pro at panic attacks and managed to control them in good time. She went out into the back garden and sat on the floor, counting her breaths. It helped her to feel grounded. She worried that the new neighbours might think she was practicing voodoo, but anything was better than a panic attack.

You're okay.
You're calm.
I can see you, anxiety.
I am safe and you need to leave.

Frankie closed her eyes and took a deep breath.

She felt better.

Recovery is a journey. You won't wake up fixed. Gentle reminders ran through her mind. Frankie knew upon first impressions nobody would think she had a problem in her mind. The cool calm demeanour. The happy go lucky outlook. The motivational mugs. Underneath it all was a delicate soul that had dealt with a lot of pain.

All along she knew that this move was going to be hard, but it seemed Cara had brought a little light into her day already. A light which lit up Frankie's dark mind.

8

Eric sat at the bar in his usual seat, rolling a cigarette from his old metal tin. '

What's with the spring in your step tonight missy?'

'Can you keep a secret?' Cara smiled as she moved closer to Eric out of earshot of the other drinkers.

'You damn well know I can.' Eric smiled as he reached for Cara's hand.

'I met a woman today. She's totally beautiful and I fancy the pants off of her!' Cara winked at Eric.

'Oh really? Surely not in Elverford?' Eric laughed.

'Yup. The problem is she's moved into Jenny's house on Elmore. I don't think I should be messing around with her tenants... should I?' Cara smiled as Eric passed him his empty lager glass for a refill.

'Sure you can. Life is for living! Don't wind up like me, married to the wrong person for your entire life. Life is too short missy.' Eric smiled, the sadness strong in his eyes again.

'Oh, Eric you do melt my heart sometimes. Have you ever thought about it... you know... telling the truth?' Cara whispered, even though the other guy at the bar was half asleep, or half dead. She couldn't quite tell.

'Pah! No way. There is no point now my dearest. It's all too late. Too little, *too late*.' Eric looked down into his old, curled up hand which grasped on to his pocket's worth of change.

'Here you go, Sir! A pint of the good stuff.' Cara smiled. As she looked passed Eric, she saw Frankie walked past the front windows. Cara felt an immediate heat rush in her cheeks again. '*Shit,* Eric! I think she's heading in now. Play it cool. DO NOT say anything.'

'Jeez. I think you need to play it cool, not me!' Eric winked and sipped his lager.

The side door swung open and Frankie walked in. She had spruced up, looking fresher than earlier. Her dark brown hair swept up, perfectly in place with a slight quiff at the front. She wore a black leather jacket that fell perfectly over her shoulders. Her dark eyes fell straight into Cara's vision.

Frankie had an inexplicable presence about her.

The good thing about the Oak was

that locals were always warming of new customers, especially new residents of Elverford. The community spirit was strong, and they wanted everyone to feel at home.

Frankie walked straight to the bar. 'Evening! I told you'd I'd come and check this place out. Have you got Jack Daniels?'

'I sure have. Thanks for coming down. This is my best customer – Eric!' Cara gestured over to Eric as she raised his glass in the air.

'Welcome to Elverford. You'll love it here.' Eric winked at Cara.

'JD and coke?' Cara swiftly moved on the conversation. Eric was at the level of merry where anything could happen.

'I'll take it was a splash of cola please.' Frankie grinned, putting a five-pound note on the bar.

'Coming right up! So, have you got yourself settled in yet?' Cara passed the drink over to Frankie and took the note.

'I sure have! Well... almost there. It's always weird moving in somewhere new.' Frankie took a seat at the bar. Cara couldn't get over her mesmerizing eyes.

'Luckily I've only done it the once. I'm planning on getting a place of my own in the next few years.'

'Ah. Don't rush. Moving ain't fun!' The JD and coke seemed to evaporate.

'I've lived in the same house for 40 years. It makes things much easier,' Eric contributed.

'I don't blame you! So what time are you working until tonight?' Frankie latched back into Cara's sight.

'I'm locking up. So really it's whenever Eric and Brian sup me dry.' Cara laughed, aware of how sad the reality of the job was.

'You lock up here on your own? Surely that's not safe for a young woman like you?' The protective tone that rode with Frankie's words made Cara feel hot.

'We're in the village now. Not that the town is that bad. You must've lived in some shit places before?'

'I sure have. Well, you know how to contact me if you need help. I don't want to go home thinking that you'll be outside of here late at night in the middle nowhere.' Frankie crossed her arms. They seemed so strong. They looked like they had worked hard in their years.

'Thank you very much. Luckily Eric sticks around to keep an eye out. He looks out for the baddies while I lock all the doors.' Cara laughed as she was already refilling Eric's next lager.

'She's a good lass. We would be in trouble without you behind this bar. Have you met the new barmaid, Lily? She is miserable. She won't let us stay late. She turfs us out as soon as she can.' Eric didn't like change.

'Oh, Eric. They're not all going to be as

good as me! I'll have a word with Dan – our *ever so helpful* boss.' Cara raised her eyebrows and slumped on one of the hand pulls. It was surprisingly quiet for a Saturday night.

'That was a great drink but I gotta go. I just wanted to show my face, but I'm shattered, as you can imagine. I mean it though, if you need me to give you a hand anytime – let me know. Really nice to meet you Cara.' Frankie's kind eyes comforted Cara as she handed over her empty glass. 'Night you two.'

Cara tilted her head and smiled.

Frankie left the bar. It took seconds until Eric pursed his lips at Cara.

'Damn, she likes you, honey! You best get her number saved. That was very brief though.'

'I doubt Jenny will be best pleased about this. And I know, she seems mysterious. I can't put my finger on it.' Cara smiled to herself. Something about Frankie excited her.

She still wasn't sure what it was yet, but she hoped to find out.

9

Jenny had returned Sunday morning from her dirty night away with Kirsty. As soon as she walked through the door she was already on the phone to Kirsty, letting her know how much she was missing her. Cara smiled at Jenny, so pleased to see her looking genuinely happy even if it was a little soppy.

Jenny ended the call and jumped on the sofa next to Cara.

'So, let me guess... you had the best sex ever last night, didn't you? It's written all over your beautiful, filthy face.' Cara smiled as she crossed over her legs to get herself comfy on the sofa.

'I sure did. I didn't know I could orgasm more than once at the same time. Of course, I've heard of the elusive multiple orgasms, however, I have never experienced them first hand. I was in heaven! Did you meet Frankie? What is she like? No creepy weird vibes?' Jenny stretched out her legs, they were sore from a night of stretching in ways she didn't know she could.

'Yes! She's... lovely. We had a brew together and then she popped down to the Oak last night. She's also kinda... hot.' Cara blushed.

Jenny immediately scrunched her eyebrows together.

'Please don't fuck my tenant.' Jenny crossed her arms, looking thoroughly unimpressed.

'I knew you'd say that. I'm not fucking anyone. I'm just saying... she's hot.'

'Yes, but she also needs to pay the rent to cover my mortgage on that house and I can't be arsed with lesbian drama – caused by you!' Jenny needed a good tenant after the last pair ruined the place and left her in financial difficulty.

'I know! Don't get arsey with me. I handed over your paperwork and it's all fine. I thought it would be good to get to know her a little better, so I could, you know, check for creepy weird vibes?' Cara laughed and poked Jenny in the ribs as if to loosen up her stern-looking face.

'Well, that's a good start at least. Right, I need a bath. My body is killing me!' Jenny squeezed Cara on the arm as she pulled herself upwards. 'I fancy a couple of drinks today if you want to join me? Shall we go to the Tavern?'

The Tavern was the other local pub just

outside of Elverford. They didn't usually venture there as it was closer to where Jenny's ex, Michelle, was living her dream life with plain boring Sue. It seemed now Jenny was lost in Kirsty and her orgasms, she was finally getting over the Michelle heartbreak.

'Sure. It's my first Sunday off in forever and *the last place* I want to be is in a pub... but as it's *you* who asked, I'll join.' Cara rolled her eyes. She wanted to help Jenny get stronger and move on from the past.

'Fantastic. I'll get sorted; we can go for an afternoon drink. I'll take the car then we can get a lift back later?' Jenny liked to take control.

'If push comes to shove, we can walk it.' Cara laughed; fully aware that Jenny despised even walking to the shop.

'Next joke.' Jenny blew a kiss to Cara and made her way upstairs.

As Cara stretched herself out on the sofa her thoughts were drifting back over to the image of Frankie. Tall, mysterious

Frankie. Her mind wondered deeply as she desperately wanted to know what was lying beneath the exterior. She imagined how her naked body would feel on top of her. Cara loved feeling overpowered by a woman. She liked to be controlled and dominated in the bedroom. A natural submissive at heart.

Cara felt herself becoming heated in between her legs. She got off the sofa and quickly made her way up to her room. She could hear that Jenny was listening to music and had the shower on so she wouldn't hear anything.

Cara got under her covers and reached into her bedside table drawer to pull out her bullet vibrator. It was so strong for such a little thing. The desire was strong as she slipped the cold vibrating metal under her trousers and pushed her underwear to the side, allowing her wetness to be exposed to the vibration. She pushed down on her clit as she rotated the bullet around her soaked centre. It was impossible not to let out a little moan. As her eyes closed, she imagined Frankie's strong fingers playing with her clit in the same circular motions as the bullet. The thought in her mind of Frankie sliding in her long fingers, filling her up and keeping her pinned down with the other hand.

She wanted Frankie's strong body to overtake her smaller frame. She wanted this stranger to fuck her life into place. With barely a minute of thought about this mysterious woman fucking her ready opening, Cara came hard, pulling at the sheet with her free hand and arching her back into the beautiful climax.

A trickle of wetness dripped down her leg onto the bed.

A small patch left beneath her on the bedsheet.

Fuck, she wanted her badly.
Frankie.

10

The Tavern was well known as a traditional, country village pub. The locals occupied the bar with their favourite stools, the fresh food scent drifted in from the kitchen and most people were on a first-name basis with each other.

As Jenny and Cara walked in, Cara noticed Jenny's eyes shoot around as she was on high alert looking out for Michelle.

Luckily, it was easy to see, there weren't many diners, all half-cut and full of Sunday dinner.

'Good evening ladies! Haven't seen you two in here for some time.' Tanya the landlady was a busty woman with a wholesome grin.

'I know! We've been busy on the other side of the river. Two pints of your finest fruity cider please.' Jenny smiled and got out her rainbow coin purse to pay.

'Coming right up.' Tanya had been in charge of the Tavern for decades and somehow managed to keep the prices as low as possible without going under.

'Shall we go and sit by the fire? I might even order some food.' Cara was excited by the smell of rich gravy floating past her nose.

'Sure honey. Whatever you like. Thanks for coming out with me.' Jenny grabbed the drinks and headed over to the wooden table by the open fire.

The pair perched on the wooden stools by the fire, taking a thirsty gulp of their drink at the same time – followed by a sigh of relief and enjoyment.

'So, remember Kirsty telling you about her single lesbian friend? How about I organise a double date?' Jenny raised her eyebrows and winked.

'Ah, I'm not sure... I don't know if I feel up for that yet.' Cara knew damn well the only thing she wanted to explore further was Frankie the unknown.

'Come on! Where's your sense of fun? It might be a laugh. You might even get laid. I still think you need it.' Jenny chuckled.

'Ah shut it! Maybe. I'll see. If there's food involved, I might be persuaded.' Cara smiled and stretched out her legs closer to the heat from the fire.

In a split second, Jenny's facial expression changed from a sarcastic smile to as if she had seen a ghost. Cara turned her head to see what she was looking at.

There stood the ghost of her past.

Michelle.

Coming out of the kitchen in chef's whites.

'What the sweet fuck is she doing working in the kitchen? What the fuck. Shit. I need to hide.' Jenny's pale complexion flushed to beetroot red as she dipped her head to avoid any contact.

'Calm down. She hasn't seen you yet. Just relax and look at me.' Cara moved her stool to block the view. It was too late. Michelle had spotted Jenny and was making her way over.

'Hey, strangers. Fancy seeing you two in here. Are you eating with us today?' Michelle smiled, with no idea just how uncomfortable Jenny felt inside.

'Hi. I know! I haven't been here in some time that's for sure. You're cooking? I mean you were always a good cook but what about your gardening? Your business?' Jenny didn't beat around the bush.

'Ah it was too stressful; I just didn't want the responsibility anymore. The last chef left, well Tanya kicked him out as she caught him shagging the waitress behind the bins. He was gross. She was looking for someone and she knew I was a keen cook. So here I am! Anyway, how are you doing?' Michelle rested one hand on the table as she leaned, placing her other hand on her hip.

'Yes, I'm great thank you. I'm dating, well I have a girlfriend. Currently in *the honeymoon* period! I'm so happy.' Jenny was trying too hard. It was painful to see.

'Oh wow! Good for you. Well, I've got news too, Sue is pregnant. I'm gonna be a baby momma, or dadda – I think that feels more comfortable.' Michelle laughed. Jenny felt her stomach drop like the heaviest weight imaginable. She once dreamed of marriage and babies with this woman.

'Congrats Michelle. I'm happy for

you,' Jenny said as her face didn't match her words.

Cara knew she had to help out.

'I am starving. I might order a roast. I can smell lamb!' Cara took the menu and started licking her lips.

'Just let Tanya know when you're ready. I best get back in the kitchen. Great to see you both. Take care, Jenny.' Michelle walked back to the kitchen, unaware of Jenny's aching pain.

'I feel sick.' Jenny did look quite pale.

'Oh Jen. Shall we go?' Cara put her hand on Jenny's arm.

'No! She won't fucking ruin my cider and my Sunday. I just can't believe it. I shouldn't still feel this hurt by it all.' Jenny looked away.

'It's okay. Time is a healer. Let's finish this and then head home. How about that?' Cara rubbed Jenny's arm in comfort.

'Maybe. Sorry, Cara. I dragged you

here and now look, drama. Let's change the subject.' Jenny put on her best fake smile.

'I think your new tenant was flirting with me. She came to the pub and I swear she was trying on the charm.' Cara knew it would take Jenny's mind off of Michelle, even if it pissed her off.

'Oh heck! Cara I don't want you to get involved with her. If things go wrong – it fucks things up with the house. I know it sounds selfish but...' Jenny wasn't up for jokes.

'I know. I'm just saying! She wants a slice. In all honesty, she is nice, and I enjoyed speaking to her. I'll keep it friendly don't worry. You're my priority.' Cara smiled and picked up her drink.

'Wow. Your eyes just lit up. This is going to be a mess if you're not careful. Why don't you just come and meet Kirsty's friend? You probably like Frankie because there are no other hot women in this place, other than me, and we could never be anything other than best mates.'

'Fine. I'll go but don't expect romance and fireworks though. I'll be polite and kind.' Cara frowned as she thought, *why the hell not?*

'Great! So, it's kind of already arranged. I knew you were free tomorrow night. We booked a table in town at 7:30 at The Olde Bell.' Jenny grinned.

'Jenny! You're a nightmare.'

'You love it and you wouldn't change me for the world. To the best of friends!' Jenny raised her glass to chink it with Cara's.

'I love you but sometimes I hate you.' Cara clinked her pint pot and squinted her eyes.

'Let's go. I'll get us a pizza tonight – my treat!' Jenny wanted to get out of the Tavern.

'What a great idea. I might just love

you a little more.' Pizza was always a great answer to some of life's trivial problems.

The pair finished their drink and made their way back home, ready for a cosy night that would consist of watching films and eating pizza.

Jenny needed to take her mind somewhere else and Cara needed to prepare for meeting a new woman tomorrow, one who disappointingly wasn't Frankie.

11

'You look hot and dangerous,' Jenny said with a Cheshire cat grin on her face and a glass of wine in her hand.

'I'm not entirely sure what that means, but I'll take it!' Cara shrugged her shoulders as she walked into the living room in a tight black dress that fitted her figure perfectly. Her blonde wavy hair was down, falling to one side. She had decided to wear a little makeup, even though her blue eyes popped out like jewels on their own. 'I just wanted to make an effort. Even if just to make myself feel good! I'm sick of smelling like a stale pub.'

'You don't have to explain yourself to me. You look great. Hopefully, you'll enjoy your blind date,' Jenny said as she looked down at her red dress and pulled it into place. 'I'm not underdressed, am I?'

'Not at all, Jen. The Olde Bell isn't exactly fancy. I just wanted to feel... good! Besides that, you always look amazing,' Cara said with a warming smile.

The doorbell rang and Jenny jumped up from the sofa, knowing it would be her beloved Kirsty who had arrived to be their chauffeur. Jenny opened the door in a hurry and planted her lips on Kirsty's friendly face as fast she could.

'I've missed you!' Jenny wrapped her arms around Kirsty and squeezed her, a little too tight.

'And I've missed you gorgeous. You look incredible – and so do you, Cara.' Kirsty was wearing her smart attire.

Ironed black trousers, a denim jacket, and a flannel shirt.

'Thank you, and I appreciate you driving us tonight. I'm looking forward to meeting your friend.' Cara was polite and didn't want to admit to anyone that the only woman she wanted to get to know further was still Frankie.

'Mel is very excited to meet you. She's nice. I think you'll like her – most people do. Anyway, shall we get going? I don't want Mel to think you've stood her up.' Kirsty laughed as she gestured her hand towards the door, 'Ladies first!'.

∽

AFTER A 30-MINUTE CAR journey into the local town, the trio arrived at The Olde Bell car park.

'I feel nervous, or sick, Cara said as she held her stomach, she wasn't sure if it was from being in the back of a car or watching Jenny and Kirsty almost have sex in the front.

'It'll be fun! Just be yourself. She'll like you.' Kirsty reassured Cara as they made their way into the pub.

As Cara walked through the door behind Kirsty, she spotted Mel straight away. She was sat by a large table on her own, awkwardly smiling in their direction.

Mel was older than Cara expected, not that it mattered to her. She had dark brown hair which was short at one side and spiked up at the top.

Mel had been single for a while now. She often scared of girls by being too full on.

Cara made her way over to her and held out her hand which Mel shook firmly, and her grin widened, and her cheeks flushed. 'Hi! I'm Cara, nice to meet you. I've heard so much about you.' Cara felt terrible. On first impressions alone, there was no initial attraction but Cara decided to give try as she believed that personality built so much attraction to a person.

'I'm Mel. *Obviously*! Nice to meet you. You look great by the way.' Mel tilted her head to the side with a giant grin on her face. Cara couldn't help but instantly compare her attraction towards Frankie against her lack of attraction for anyone else. Frankie instantly made her excited. Mel instantly made her turned off.

'Ah thank you, so do you.' Cara replied. Mel did look nice. She had made an effort. Her hair was perfectly spiked up into place. She wore tight black jeans and a dark green Ralph Lauren jumper. Her brown eyes widened as she looked Cara up and down, admiring her hourglass figure that was perfectly highlighted by her tight black dress.

'What are you two having to drink? We will go and order.' Jenny was great at breaking awkwardness.

'I'll have cider please, anything fruity.' Cara smiled, trying to stop her thoughts from swaying over to Frankie again.

'I'll have a vodka and coke, please! Just a single though, I don't want to get carried away.' Mel winked at Cara and sat down.

'So, what do you?' Cara wanted to steer the conversation into normal territory. Fast.

'I'm a mechanic. I work in town at Mumby's garage. If you ever need work doing, you know where to come.' Mel meant well, but she tried hard. Too hard. All of the time.

The truth behind it was that she was desperate to love someone and give them her all.

'I've been there 20 years now. What do you do? Let me guess... you're a model.'

Cara internally cringed.

'Ha, no. Nothing too exotic. I'm a barmaid in Elverford at the Oak. I don't plan on staying there forever but it's not that bad.'

'Ah, nice. I'll have to check it out sometime.' Mel smiled, trying not to let the conversation die prematurely.

Luckily Kirsty and Jenny had arrived with drinks for everyone.

'Hey mate. How's your day been?' Kirsty asked Mel as she sipped on her pint of real ale.

'Not bad thank you! I managed to scrub the grease out of my hands from work. I wanted to scrub up for a pub meal, especially in the company of fine women.' Mel giggled and nudged Cara.

'Ah, hopefully, it'll be good! Jenny, I just need to use the toilet, fancy joining me?' Cara scrunched her face and smiled at Jenny. It was code facial expressions that meant *say yes and join me.*

'Sure. Excuse us!' Jenny stood up, pulled down her red dress, which was a little too short and tight-fitting.

Kirsty liked the view.

The pair made their way into the toilet and Cara rushed over to the sink.

'I can't do this Jenny.'

'We've only just got here! Chill out, woman.' Jenny looked in the mirror and reapplied her dark red matte lipstick.

'I don't fancy her at all. I'm cringing. This was a bad idea.' Cara sighed.

'Just relax. We can enjoy our meal, have a few drinks then go. Don't make it awkward please.'

'Eugh. I didn't want to be here in the first place.' Cara snapped.

'Don't get moody with me missy. I was just trying to do a nice thing. Maybe Mel will get better with the night, or after a few drinks.' Jenny laughed.

'I mean, she seems lovely and everything, but I'm just not attracted to her and the more she talks the less I fancy her. Sorry, my mind is elsewhere. Love you mate.' Cara wrapped her arms around Jenny.

'Do you want to talk about it?' Jenny said as she squeezed Cara in closer.

As Cara looked up and closed her eyes, she saw Frankie looking back at her and smiling with her beautiful mouth.

This couldn't go on much longer.

She had to think of a way to see her soon.

'No, it's fine. Let's go back out there. I just freaked out a bit when she winked at me and looked me up and down like a hot meal. We can have food, have a laugh, and go home later. Please don't leave me alone with her for too long okay? I don't want to make false, flirtatious conversation all night.'

'Don't worry, I won't.' Jenny pulled away from the hug and straightened out her dress one more time. 'Damn thing keeps riding up! Come on, let's go back.'

Cara linked Jenny's arm as they made

their way back to the table. Kirsty and Mel were sat waiting eagerly like happy little puppies.

'How lucky are we to be joined by these two beautiful women?' Mel said to Kirsty as she held her drink in the air.

'Very lucky.' Kirsty laughed. She was fully aware of Mel's terrible flirting. She had known her for years.

Cara and Jenny laughed as they sat back down in their seats, both grabbing a menu hoping it might speed things up a little.

'I think I'll have a steak, or maybe surf 'n' turf.' Cara's eyes lit up as she made her way through the menu. It was such a treat not to be the one taking the order or carrying out the food.

'Surely a *little lady* like yourself can't eat an entire surf 'n' turf?' Mel asked Cara as she gulped down her drink.

Jenny closed her eyes and frowned.

She could tell by Cara's facial expression that she was a woman on the edge.

'I'm quite capable. Thank you.' Cara smiled sarcastically as she put down the menu.

Mel didn't quite understand the sarcasm as she laughed to herself.

'I think I'll have a chicken burger, and I might go for a cig. If the waitress comes while I'm outside will you tell her for me?' Mel smiled at Kirsty as she pulled out her tobacco pouch and started rolling a cigarette.

'Sure,' Cara replied.

'Thanks. Anyone else want to join me?' Mel looked around the table awaiting a smoking buddy.

'I will!' Jenny grinned as she pulled out her pack of cigarettes from her bright red clutch bag.

Cara clocked Kirsty as she rolled her eyes. She hated it when Jenny tasted like an ashtray. She knew that if Jenny was ever going to quit smoking it had to be her own decision.

Jenny didn't like being told what to do.

'Perfect!'

Mel said as she stood up and followed Jenny into the smoking area.

'Are you okay? You seem a little quiet. I'm sorry if this is awkward. I know Mel is quite full on – believe me I've seen her worse than this.' Kirsty laughed.

'If I'm being completely honest my mind is elsewhere. I met Jenny's new tenant and I just can't stop thinking about her. I know I sound like a crazy woman, but she had an impact on me.' Cara felt comfortable opening up to Kirsty, she had that effect on people.

'Well, what's stopping you?' Kirsty leaned forward, listening intently.

'Jenny. She doesn't want me getting *involved* with her tenant, she's worried about the *lesbian drama*.'

'She'll get over it. You've got to do what makes you happy Cara. Life is too short.' Kirsty picked up her pint pot and finished her drink.

'Thanks, Kirsty. I think you're right.' Cara smiled.

She had nothing to lose, and life was too short.

Cara had her mind focussed on one person.

A stranger.

The strange woman in Elmore Street.

Frankie.

12

'I guess you're not interested in seeing Mel again then? I thought last night was fun regardless of the incompatibility. Well, I think she fell in love with you, but you clearly weren't bothered,' Jenny said as she was spreading herself out across the sofa, one of her favourite places to be.

'I'll be polite and civil if I was to see her again but... romantically it's a *no* from me. Thanks for trying though.' Cara was sat in the armchair. Her legs crossed and covered in a fluffy blanket.

Cara was pleased that Kirsty hadn't told Jenny about her forbidden feelings.

'At least you got out somewhere different. Do you like Kirsty? Do I have your approval?' Jenny turned down the volume and shuffled herself up into a seated position.

'She's wonderful Jen. I think she's so nice. I'm really happy for you.' Cara smiled.

'I'm happy too. I think I've fallen in love.'

'I think you might be right! Seriously I'm happy. You look content with her. She's a good person. Oh Jen, I really can't be bothered with work today.' Cara sighed as she thought about the woman on her mind and the lack of motivation to pull another pint.

'I bet. I am so glad I booked this annual leave.' Jenny turned to face the television again. She worked in a care home, usually doing 3 long days a week. Jenny was a great support worker with her genuine love and care for every single resident.

As Cara slumped into the armchair, her thoughts drifted as she began to think about how she could see Frankie without it too seeming strange, or full-on, like Mel.

Maybe Frankie would turn up to her work again.

Maybe she could walk to work via her house and see if she was around.

Surely there was a way of seeing her. Was she being crazy?

Cara knew that there could be a chance Frankie liked her too.

Like Eric said that night in the pub. She was flirting.

Cara looked up at the clock and realised she had an hour left before work to start at 4 pm.

'I best get ready.' After a long sigh,

Cara managed to get herself out of the armchair.

'Good luck. I'll probably still be here when you get back. I'm ordering in, I'll save you some food,' Jenny said as was still facing the television.

'You're the best,' Cara replied as she made her way upstairs to get ready.

~

THE PUB SEEMED MORE quiet than usual, even for a Tuesday. Eric and a few other locals were slumped and drinking as usual. It seemed like the longest shift ever, which Cara spent mainly deep cleaning the bar and chatting to one of the waitresses.

As Cara polished the hand pull, she noticed a familiar figure walking past the window. It was Frankie. Cara's stomach dropped.

'Oh, I forgot to tell you. Your lady

friend was in yesterday, she asked me when you were next working.' Eric smiled at Cara, knowing full well he had set this up on purpose.

Cara didn't have time to reply as Frankie was already halfway inside and making her way to the bar.

She could feel the blood fill her cheeks. Anxiety and butterflies overtook her body.

Act cool. Stay calm. Cara's mind repeated over and over.

'Hey, you! A pint of your finest ale, please. How've you been?' Frankie sat down on the barstool and took off her light blue denim jacket. Her deep eyes made Cara desire to stare into her soul.

'Hey. Yes of course. I'm doing well, thank you. How are you doing?' Cara was trying her best to act normal, but also to not seem cold due to her nerves taking over her entire body still.

'Yes, grand thanks. I was hoping to

catch you! It's my birthday at the weekend, I'm thinking about having some friends over on Friday. I know it sounds weird, but I wanted to invite you and Jenny. You two are my first friends around here. You can come too if you like Eric. I also wanted to check Jenny wouldn't mind me having a little soiree. I haven't even met the woman in person yet!' Frankie had such an alluring aura.

'Oh, sure yeah. That would be great. I'm working until 9 pm next Friday so I can swing by afterwards, and Jenny wouldn't mind at all.' Cara leaned on the bar, her low-cut top showing off her cleavage. She felt Frankie's eyes scan over her breasts.

'Amazing. I'm only having a few people over. I'll be making food so save some room for a buffet! Can you let Jenny know for me? And if she has someone that she wants to bring that's fine, and the same goes to you.' Frankie gulped her pint as she ran her fingers through her hair.

'Yeah, she might bring her girlfriend Kirsty. I don't have anyone I would bring, other than Eric.' Cara laughed, hoping to drill her relationship status in Frankie.

'Great. It'll be good! Are you on until close tonight?' Frankie was keen to chat.

'Yes, unfortunately. It seems pretty quiet though so I hope I can get away about 11,' Cara said as she looked at Eric.

'You better not turf me out any earlier than that!' Eric said with stern eyes.

Cara rolled her eyes and smiled. She did love Eric, but he was often the last punter in the place. She felt too polite to turf him out, and occasionally he'd remind her of the pub's license to serve until midnight.

'Anyway, how's your weekend been? Have you been up to much?' Frankie asked as she crossed her arms across the bar. They were toned and sun-kissed. Cara longed for them to pin her down.

'Well actually, Jenny set me up with a date last night, a double date. It was awful!' Cara wondered if she could gauge a reaction from Frankie. She still wasn't entirely sure if her attraction was reciprocated.

Frankie frowned as she smiled at Cara, was she pleased that it didn't go well? Hopefully.

'Sorry to hear that! What was so bad about it?'

'You know when you meet someone and there is just no spark. So much so that it felt like I disliked the poor woman. She was alright but just made me cringe with her full-on flirting. She tried to deny me of a Surf 'n' Turf because she thought I couldn't handle it.' Cara laughed and put her palm to her forehead.

Frankie smiled, 'Oh dear. Even I can

tell you can handle it. So, you won't be going back for a second date then?'

'Not a chance. How about you? Have you got anyone on the scene?' Cara could tell Eric was judging her poor effort to flirt with Frankie.

'Nope. I've been single for some time now. Who knows what's around the corner though?' Frankie finished her drink and put on her jacket. It seemed that any personal questions were soon diverted. Cara felt her stomach drop. She didn't want her to leave so soon.

'I best be going. Up early tomorrow sorting out someone's garden down the road! If I don't see you beforehand, see you on Friday. Bye guys!'

'Yes. I'll be there.' Cara tilted her head slightly as she smiled watching Frankie leave. Surely, she knew that she wanted her on some level.

'You two need to just get it on already. I could've cut the tension with a blunt knife.' Eric raised his eyebrows and smirked.

'You're right Eric. We do.'

Cara spent the entire shift conjuring up a plan. She needed to make a move. Any kind of move. Even if Jenny disagreed with it, she wasn't really harming anybody. Life is far too short to deny one's self of passion and great sex. She could already tell that the sex would be great with Frankie, or at least it was in her mind.

13

Friday had finally arrived, and Cara had managed to swap her shift at work to get the full day off. She hoped this would give her enough time to get ready properly for Frankie's party.

She wanted Frankie to think that she looked good. This feeling in her stomach reminded her of having a crush on her teacher at school. The giddy excitement filling her mind as the fantasies passed through. Each one more intense than the last. Cara felt like a starved animal ready to eat.

'I hope you enjoy yourself tonight. I can't remember the last time I went to any kind of party. Maybe we should have one here soon,' Jenny said as she packed up her bag to go away for the night with Kirsty.

'I can't wait! I hope you two enjoy yourselves, I'm jealous of you and your dirty nights away.' Cara laughed as she put one hand on her hip.

'Well, it could've been you and Mel. You missed your chance honey.' Jenny chuckled as she stood up and hugged Cara. 'See you on Sunday. Don't do anything stupid.'

'I can't make those kinds of promises,' Cara said fully aware of her plan to push her luck with Jenny's tenant.

Jenny sighed, smiled, and then left the front door. Cara made her way to the kitchen and grabbed her 4 pack of beers to take with her to the party. She had already spent hours getting ready. It took her at least half an hour to find the right clothes to wear. Tight black jeans and a fitted top with her favourite denim jacket. She knew it would be an informal dress and Cara hated overdressing for an occasion.

∽

CARA ARRIVED at Frankie's house which seemed unusually quiet for a party. She made her way to the front door and eagerly knocked. The house looked empty through the front window. *Maybe people are running late*, Cara thought to herself.

Frankie opened the front door and had barely half a smile upon her face. 'Hey, thanks for coming. You look so lovely.'

'Thanks. As do you and happy birthday!' Cara said as she admired Frankie's long muscular legs in tight blue denim. 'It seems pretty quiet for a birthday party?'

'Ha, thanks. It's not until tomorrow! It's quiet because my *so-called* friends let me down. It wouldn't be the first time.' Frankie looked down at the floor and she gestured with her hand for Cara to come inside. She needed the company.

'You're joking? What kind of friends are they? As if they all let you down. I'm sorry Frankie.' Cara walked into the house and saw through the living door window that Frankie had prepared a feast enough for at least 20 people.

'They're pretty flakey friends. I hope you're hungry!' Frankie laughed, she tried to find the humour in the situation

'I actually am. Well, we can have a fun time. If you're still up for a little party with me.' Cara turned and smiled at Frankie. She felt so sad for her. Her eyes looked drowned with sadness. To Cara it seemed really bizarre that *none* of her friends could make it, but without second questioning it, she delved into her bag and got out a card and present. Cara had found a little 10 in 1 tool with an assortment of handy things on it. Cara wasn't so sure what they were all for but it seemed fitting for Frankie.

'Oh Cara, you didn't have to do that. Thank you.' Frankie put her hand on Cara's arm as she spoke softly.

'It's fine. How could I turn up to a party without a present? Shall we have a drink? I bought beer too.'

Frankie put her card and present on the side and nodded her head as she grabbed the beers from Cara and popped them open with her new 10 in 1 tool.

'Here you go. What a great gift!' Frankie passed the beer over, her eyes meeting Cara's. The moment felt longer than it should've, but Frankie dismissed it as she looked away and drank her beer.

Cara smiled back as she took a drink.

'You've got the house looking so nice already. The last tenants ruined the place for Jenny.'

'Really? Some people are such idiots. I like to keep myself busy. Some would say I'm a human doing and not a human being. Would you like to sit in the living room? It's comfier in there. In reality I am thirty-five tomorrow and I'm not afraid to say that I choose comfort over style,' Frankie laughed to herself.

'Sure.' Cara made her way through the hallway and into the living room. The buffet and balloons made her heart sink.

'I think I'll need to take some of this to the pub for people to eat! I'll never get through it all here on my own.' Frankie sighed.

'If you plate it up, I can take it to the bar with me tomorrow. The old boys at the bar would hoover it up.' Cara scrunched up her nose as she sat back into the sofa. She felt so nervous. Frankie looked so good, even though she was a little sad.

Everything about her was attractive to Cara.

The laughter lines when she smiled.

The cracks in her hard-working hands.

'Are you okay? You don't have to stick around here with me you know. I understand if you want to leave after this drink. It's not much of a party. I'm a boring sod really.'

'I'm not going anywhere. Surely you've experienced a two-person party before?'

Frankie looked up as she was trying to recall the last time that she had fun. Cara found it strange that she seemed so isolated. It was like she was hiding something.

Either way, she wanted to find out.

Frankie looked at Cara and smiled.

'Honestly, the last time was years ago. I can't even remember. I really appreciate you coming over here though, it's so lovely to spend time with you.'

'Well I'm free all night so maybe we can do one.' And that's not the only thing Cara wanted to do.

'Luckily, my diary is completely empty.' Frankie said as she sat across from Cara. 'Shall I play some music?'

'Sure! I'll listen to anything.' Cara stood up and made her way over to the CD rack. She liked the fact that Frankie had CDs. It seemed so *old school* now.

She turned around with a Tracy Chapman album in her hand to realise that Frankie was stood directly behind her. Cara looked up, immediately latching on to the desire in Frankie's eyes. Her heart fluttered. Her cheeks flushed. Nervous hands slid down by her sides. Her body's response took over everything without a moment of thought. Frankie leaned in to kiss her. It was a kiss that lingered as their tongues met slowly. Cara placed the album on the table and put her hand on Frankie's side. Frankie pulled her lips away and pushed her forehead gently against Cara's, taking her wrist and holding it back towards the wall.

'It's my birthday, and I know what I want,' Frankie said with a heavy breath.

Cara could feel the blood pulsating in her core as she gently exhaled. 'And what is it that you want?'

'I want to be inside of you. I have since the moment I met you.' Frankie was panting with excitement as she pushed Cara back into the wall, taking her breath away.

The dynamic between them was evident from the start. Nobody needed to say anything. Frankie was dominant and Cara wanted to submit, completely.

'I'm glad that you know your manners,' Frankie whispered, pushing her hand harder through Cara's jeans. 'I want you to bend over. Put your hands on the sofa over there and wait for me to come back.'

Without hesitation, Cara took a deep breath and walked over of the sofa where she happily bent over, supporting herself by the sofa.

Frankie ran upstairs.

She wasn't sure what she was waiting for, but there were no complaints.

Frankie came down the stairs and went back into the living room. 'Good girl, Cara. Keep your eyes shut and stay where you are.' As Frankie walked up behind her Cara gasped as she felt something hard brush against her behind. 'You don't mind this do you?' Frankie said as she put her hands around Cara's hips and pulled her hips closer to the strap on which she was wearing.

All Frankie had on was the leather harness and a thick, 8-inch shaft.

Cara could've fallen to the floor in excitement. This was everything she wanted and more. 'I have no problem at all.' She expressed willingly.

Frankie put her hands around Cara's front and unbuttoned her jeans to pull them down halfway. As Cara bent over, her black lace underwear was exposed. Frankie's eye lit up. She moved closer, allowing the strap on to slip in between Cara's thighs, brushing against her wetness.

Cara immediately moaned.

She wanted this.

So desperately.

'Does that feel good? Are you ready to take it?' Frankie was at home in all senses.

'I will take anything.' Cara pushed back, eager for more,

As Frankie smirked, she ran her finger across the black lace and pushed it up to the side. Even the tension from the underwear pulling against Cara's clit made her gasp. Frankie held the shaft in one hand, and teased it in, slowly filling Cara with the thickness and length. Cara's heart was pounding with excitement as she let out a deep moan, feeling stretched and full. Frankie pulled back and began to fuck her slow and deep, aware of how soaking wet Cara had become, grabbing her hips and pulling her in deeper each time. Each thrust was filled with deeper moans. Frankie increased the power, fucking her as hard as she could take it, enjoying every single movement. The leather strap brushed against Frankie's clit, bringing her to climax sooner than she anticipated. She was so turned on by Cara. The desire was overtaking her control. Frankie let out a moan as pushed deeper inside, forcing Cara to cum at the same time. The wetness dripping out and down her legs. Her pulsating core throbbing with excitement. The living room filled with sex and passion. Frankie bent over the top of Cara and left a moment for them to breathe heavily in each other's sex.

'That was fucking insane,' Cara said as she slumped into the sofa and tried to pull her jeans back up a little. Frankie took off the harness and laid with her. Stroking her back and hair.

'You are wonderful Cara.'

'So are you. You really are.'

As they positioned themselves into a spooning position on the sofa, their bodies entwined as they bathed in the moment of post-sex bliss. Frankie kissed Cara on the nape of her neck sending shivers throughout her body. The night had drawn in and in the comfort of each other, they fell asleep.

14

Frankie opened her eyes and looked up at the living room clock to realise it was past midnight. Cara was still curled up in front of her sleeping. She looked so peaceful and calm. Frankie couldn't believe they had been asleep for so long. She put it down to the stress and the orgasms. As gentle as she could, she took her arm from around Cara's body and got herself off of the sofa without disturbing her. After a glance around the living room, she noticed some clean washing on the side and got some clothes on. The house has turned quite chilly. Frankie looked over at Cara. The lovely Cara lying on her sofa. Her thick hair draped down the side of her face. Plump pink lips slightly parted as she snoozed. Ever since the moment Frankie laid eyes on her kind face, she knew she wanted more.

Frankie wasn't one for opening herself up to anyone too easily and she had her reasons.

∼

She liked Cara, a lot. Her heart had warmed up after years frozen like a lump of meat in the bottom shelf of the freezer. As terrifying as it seemed, she knew she would have to be honest with her. Share her secrets. Better sooner than later, especially as her feelings were growing every second, she admired Cara's serene sleeping face.

The sofa was comfy, but not good enough for a decent sleep. Frankie tenderly put her hand on Cara's shoulder, 'Hey, wake up, pretty girl. Let's get you to bed,' Frankie spoke gently.

Cara peeled open one eye surprised that she had slept so soundly. 'Oh my god, what time is it? Was that sex real or another filthy dream of mine?'

Franke laughed and kissed Cara on the forehead. 'I hope it was real. It's late. Are you hungry? Or just want to go to bed?'

'Happy birthday to you, by the way! I wouldn't want to turn up to a party and not enjoy any of the buffet, especially as nice as it looks. I think I could grab some snacks before bed, couldn't I?' Cara smirked as she slowly got off of the sofa, wrapped in a blanket. She reached over for a plate and uncovered some of the snacks on the table. 'Cheese and onion roll! Perfect.'

Frankie was desperate to open up about her past life events, but she knew it wasn't the right time.

The poor girl was half asleep and enjoying the birthday buffet food

So, for now, all Frankie could do was smile at Cara's endearing nature.

Cara scrunched up her face and returned the smile.

15

The next morning, Cara opened her slumberous eyes and noticed Frankie was nowhere to be seen. A sudden dread overtook her body. *Where has she gone? Did she regret what happened?* The thoughts surged in Cara's mind like an insubordinate tornado. As she became aware of her unfamiliar surroundings, she noticed a smell drifting through the air. A moment later, she heard Frankie making her way up the stairs. When she made it to the top, Cara could see she was holding a tray with breakfast goods and fresh orange juice.

'It's your birthday! Not mine!' Cara blushed. Nobody had ever brought her breakfast in bed.

'Well you are the best present I could wish for.' Frankie laughed as she placed the tray down on the bed and kissed Cara's soft plump lips.

'You're so sweet. Are you eating? There is a lot here just for me,' Cara said as she looked down at the tray filled with croissants, fresh fruit, and cuts of ham and cheese. 'Fresh coffee too, you know how to spoil a girl.'

'Oh yes. Of course, I am. I do like good coffee. I thoroughly enjoyed spoiling you last night.' Frankie smiled as her thoughts took her back to Cara's perfect form bending over her sofa. She took a croissant filled with butter and jam and enjoyed the first crisp bite, accompanied by a look of pure glee.

'Believe me, I feel truly spoiled,' Cara said as she shuffled up in the bed and admired every bit of effort that Frankie had made.

'Good. Maybe after breakfast, you could give me another birthday present?' Frankie's eyebrows raised, as she looked at Cara with desire.

'Anything you want.' Cara's smile beamed as she enjoyed the fresh coffee and fruit.

Frankie looked at her, aware of how peaceful she felt. At the same time, if she looked too hard, it was a terrifying reality of liking someone again, with the slightest chance it might make her vulnerable. The realisation hit her that she would have to open up after hiding in a cave. The biggest thought in her mind was the uncertainty of how vulnerable she could be. She looked down at her phone and panicked at the thought. Having sex was one thing, but the feelings were another. Something changed within Frankie.

'Actually, I completely forgot I have to go and pick up some work supplies today. I might have to go sooner rather than later.'

'Oh, but it's your birthday. Surely you can have the day off.' Cara could feel a sense of panic radiating from Frankie. The same rushing feeling she saw in her in the pub.

'The company I used are shut tomorrow, so I've arranged to get some bits today. Sorry. You can stay if you want and I'll just head out and get them.' Frankie got out of bed and started getting dressed.

'No, it's fine, I'll head off. You have things to do and I don't want to get in your way!' Cara finished her coffee and grabbed her clothes.

'Ok well, we can meet up soon. Maybe you could come over with Jenny for a drink, it would be good to meet her.'

Frankie buttoned up her shirt and was fully aware she was acting like a weird prick and that she was probably blowing all of her chances.

'Sure. Just give me a text some time.' Cara felt hurt.

'Of course, I will.' Frankie walked over to Cara and kissed her slowly.

Every time she touched her the worries dissipated.

Frankie handed her the spare key as she put on her jacket.

Only time will tell - Cara thought to herself as she watched Frankie leave. She got herself dressed, grabbed some breakfast goods, and made her way out - it would be rude to waste.

16

Later that day Cara was sitting at home, sprawled out on her bed reading the latest lesbian romance release. Reading was one of her favourites things to do. She found it a great way to escape from reality and lose herself in another world. Her phone vibrated, making her jump back into reality. She expected to see Dan's name flash on her phone, begging her to go into work and save the day so he didn't actually have to do anything. Cara raised her eyebrows as she saw Frankie's name on the screen.

. . .

Hey, sorry about rushing off. I get stressed when I have things on my mind. I'm not great at talking sometimes. If you want to come over with Jenny later for a drink so she can have a 'meet the tenant' experience, then you're more than welcome. Frankie x

Cara smiled to herself but then she realised one thing. She had to tell Jenny that they were fucking. Before she had time to even think about how to do that, Cara sighed as she could hear the front door opening, followed by Jenny giggling like a giddy school girl with Kirsty.

Shit.

I'll just be straight forward.

Jenny always knows when I'm lying.

Cara's mind knew what was best. She made her way downstairs and took a deep breath.

'Hey, guys! Did you have a good night?' Cara stood sheepishly, trying to act cool.

'We had a great night, although we did get a noise complaint in the hotel, that was technically Kirsty's fault.' Jenny chuckled as she looked at Kirsty and blushed. 'How was your night? Was the party good? Tell me you've kept the boundaries in place with your new friend and my new tenant.'

Kirsty knew something was about to happen, she quickly made her way into the kitchen to put the kettle on and get out of the way.

Cara didn't say anything, but the complexion of her cheeks told Jenny everything she needed to know.

'You are a fucking nightmare. You fucked, didn't you?' Jenny shouted as Cara stood sheepishly like a scared child.

'Yes. I'd rather be honest with you. I will not lie,' Cara said, avoiding eye contact.

'So, fucking my tenant – which is the *one* thing I requested for you *not* to do

– seemed like the right idea, did it?' Jenny stood confrontationally with her hand on her hips as Kirsty was in the kitchen making tea, taking as long as she could to avoid the drama.

'Yes. It did. All I can say is I'm truly sorry, but I do like her Jen and life is too short,' Cara said looking over in Kirsty's direction mercifully, hoping she might help her out.

'I feel annoyed, but whatever. If you like her then you can't help it. I just didn't want tension tied up in that house again.' Jenny crossed her arms.

'I know, and I am truly sorry. I promise if anything goes wrong I will avoid drama at all costs. No more drama on Elmore Street, just orgasms.' Cara giggled and Jenny couldn't help but raised her eyebrows and smirk.

'I did say you needed to get laid and I was right. You seem less rigid...'

'See! It's a good thing.' Cara crept

closer towards Jenny for a hug which was welcomed with open arms. 'I hate it when you're mad at me.'

'I hate it when you go against my words, but I love you still you, idiot.' Jenny squeezed harder just as Kirsty was walking in with drinks for everyone.

Thank goodness, you've made up. The tension was too much for me!' Kirsty laughed as she managed to put the balanced mugs of tea down on the side table.

'What I want to know is, when can we meet her? I feel pretty terrible I haven't met my new tenant yet, but I feel even worse now that you're sleeping with her.'

'Well I am off tonight, and I thought maybe we could go for a drink together? Frankie has invited you both over if you'd like to go there. See what she's done with the place.' Cara smiled, eager to smooth it all over.

'Why the hell not? It'll be good to see

the house.' Jenny sat down on the sofa and took her mug of tea.

'Sure thing. I'm up for it!' Kirsty joined Jenny on the sofa and Cara let out a sigh of relief.

She hated drama.

∼

LATER THAT DAY they arrived at Frankie's house with a few beers and more positivity. Cara opened the door with the spare key which Frankie had given her and called inside.

There were a few lights on, but no sign on Frankie.

The house was lifeless.

'Erhm, this is weird,' Jenny said as she took in the peculiar silence of the house.

'Let me try and ring her.' Cara pulled her phone out of her pocket and rang Frankie.

Straight to voicemail. 'This is very

weird. Maybe she's just nipped to the shop?'

'Girls, why don't we just head back home and leave her a message to let us know when she's back?' Kirsty said attempting to calm the suspicious duo.

'You two go, I'll stay here. I want to have a better look around the house and maybe I'll nip to the pub to see if she thought we were meeting her there,' Cara wasn't going anywhere. She began to panic that maybe Frankie had freaked out about what happened.

'Are you sure?' Jenny didn't mind heading home. The wintry air was ice-like and she didn't fancy sitting around waiting all night.

'Of course, get yourselves home and I'll keep you updated.'

'Ok. See you later!' Jenny and Kirsty made their way home.

Cara put all of the lights on and slowly made her way up the stairs. For some reason, she felt a little apprehensive, as if she were in a horror film about to uncover a murder – hoping it she wouldn't trip over Frankie's body on the way. Upstairs seemed quiet too. Each room was empty. No Frankie anywhere. Cara made her way back downstairs and had a look in the back garden. The only thing she saw was an empty crate of beer. Maybe Frankie had cold feet, got drunk, and evacuated? Cara's thoughts spiralled. The only place she could think to go next was the pub.

After locking the front door, Cara heard something. She walked around to see what it was, it sounded like it was coming from near the bins down the side of the house. Even though it was dark she could make out a figure sat down in the alleyway.

'Frankie, is that you? What are you doing there?' Cara put on her phone torch and moved closer.

'I'm sorry Cara. I wasn't ready. I can't

go through with this.' Frankie was slumped down by the wall wrapping her arms around her legs. This didn't seem like the same Frankie she saw yesterday. It was as if someone else had taken over her body. She was pale.

Maybe she really was a murderer.

'Not ready for what? Are you okay? You're worrying me.' Cara knelt by her side gravely concerned and unsure of who this version of Frankie was.

'These feelings. It's a lot. I need to talk to you properly because you don't really know me. I need to tell you about who I am,' Frankie said as she made eye contact and slowly pulled herself up off of the floor. She was drunk, and it must've been from the empty crate of lager. Her breath was tainted by bitter alcohol. Hey body swayed slightly as she moved.

Cara's stomach dropped. It appeared that Frankie had well and truly freaked out. 'You can talk to me about anything.

Come on, let's go inside it's freezing,' Cara said as she offered out her hand, which was rejected.

As they made their way back into the house Cara flicked up the heating and the lamps in the living room. 'Sit down I'll make us a drink. I think you need some water.'

Frankie slumped into the sofa and it was only in the light that Cara could tell how red her eyes looked. She looked as if she had cried all day.

'What has happened to you? Please talk to me.' Cara sat next to her and took her hand, passing her the glass of water.

'I don't want you to freak out about this. I'm scared of feeling... abandoned again. I lost everything once and I'm just trying to be me again.' Frankie was struggling to maintain eye contact. It became evident to Cara that something deeper was going on. Something painful.

'Please, just talk to me about whatever

it is you're feeling. There is something between us, something that took me by surprise, but I want to get to know the real you. We barely know each other, yet it feels so right to be close to you, and I feel so eager to know more. Whatever it is, you can tell me.' Cara squeezed Frankie's hand. 'We all have a past Frankie.'

'That's what I worry about – you knowing the *real me*. I come across confident but it's often just a front. You think I know what I want, but I'm... complex.' Frankie looked down at her hands as another tear fell down her cheek. 'I used to be married to a woman who I loved more than myself. She was my heaven, earth and everything in between.'

'That's okay, we all have a past. What happened between you both?' Cara felt like the layers of mystery were peeling away.

'She died. It was a terrible car accident. A guy driving a lorry went into her. I should've gone to the shops that day, but I sent her because I wasn't feeling well, and she fucking died. They couldn't save her, and it absolutely broke me, Cara. I lost my mind.' Frankie's tears strolled down her cheeks; Cara held her closer.

'I'm so sorry, that is so terrible. I don't even have the words to express how sorry I am for you.' Cara pulled Frankie into her chest and comforted her, but Frankie resisted staying there too long.

'When she died, I couldn't cope anymore. I fell into a deep dark place. My mental health fell apart and I ended up being sectioned. Have you heard of that? I was in a psychiatric ward and it was scary because I didn't know who I was anymore. I used to be fearless. I went away for months to recover; I'm still recovering now. I don't want you to think I'm crazy or dangerous. I don't want to get close to another woman just to lose them again,' Frankie said as she wiped her eyes.

'Frankie. I see you for who you and your past doesn't define you. You came into my life and took me by surprise from the moment I met you. Please don't worry about losing me. If you want to tell me about your past, I want to listen but don't ever worry about me judging you. I understand mental health. My mother has had a community mental health nurse in the past. She's been a poorly woman and thinking about – she still is. I know this small village is small minded but I promise you I am not.' Cara said with warm words as she kissed Frankie on the cheek.

'You have warmed my heart, Cara.' Frankie looked into her eyes and a smile came over her sad face. 'I thought you would realise the truth and freak out. I thought you might think it's too much baggage to take on and leave me. I'm sorry I judged you for that. I never thought anyone would understand. When my friends didn't turn up to my birthday, I knew it's because they can't see me for the person I used to be anymore. They just think I'm going to breakdown at any given moment. I've spent so much time working on myself and my own happiness. That's the real reason I moved out of here, to start somewhere fresh again. To build a new version of myself.'

'It's understandable and scary, but I will never judge you. You have a beautiful, kind soul and it's obvious to me. I can see that above anything else. Take a deep breath and relax, I'll make us a tea.' At that moment Cara already felt like she had fallen for Frankie.

She knew she loved her already on some level.

'Thank you,' Frankie replied as she leaned over and wrapped her arms around Cara. After letting out a long sigh, she pulled her close and kissed her softly.

She hadn't been this open with anybody in years.

'I really need to get a shower and then maybe you'd like to stay the night with me? I can't believe you've seen me in such a mess.'

'I sure would. Don't you worry yourself. I won't run off whilst your cleansing!' Cara smiled as she kissed Frankie once more.

After she left the room Cara got out her phone and pulled up a text conversation with Jenny.

Cara: *Hey Jen, all good here. Frankie was running late from the shop, but we got carried away so probably best to rearrange. I'll see you tomorrow x*

Jenny: *No problem, I thought as much so we're already in bed. Night x*

Cara smiled at her phone as she switched it off and pushed back into her pocket before making her way upstairs. The door to the bathroom was open as steam drifted out from the hot shower.

'Are you enjoying yourself in there?'

Frankie opened the glass shower door and leaned out, 'It'd be better if you were to join me.'

Persuasion wasn't necessary. Cara took off her clothes and got into the hot shower. Her full breasts pressing against Frankie's soft skin. She smiled as their bodies slid against each other. Frankie ran her hands around Cara's waist and pulled her close, she loved the feeling of her breasts pushing against skin. Cara looked up and kissed Frankie hard. As their tongues met, Frankie slipped her hand in between Cara's thighs and noticed the wetness as she fingers slid against her.

'You turn me on so much,' Cara moaned.

'As do you. Part your legs for me,' Frankie said in a stern voice. 'What I am sure of is how much I like what a good girl you are for me.'

'Always,' Cara replied as she lifted one leg, leaning her foot on the side of the shower.

Frankie slid her hands all around Cara's hot core. Teasing her. Lightly pinching her clit. Slowly rolling her fingers all over her wetness before pushing her fingers inside and taking Cara's breath away. Frankie curled her fingers up, hitting Cara's sweet spot continuously. Pounding away at her desire. Cara felt her body jerk. Her climax building intensely. Frankie picked up the speed whilst putting her other hand around Cara's thigh, adding more power to the fucking. Cara melted in a wet orgasm as Frankie kept her fingers deep inside for a moment longer, enjoying the way she clenched around them. Cara looked into her eyes as she bit her lip. Enjoying every second of her body pulsating.

Frankie kissed her lips. 'May I wash your body?'

'Of course. Nobody has ever washed me before.' Cara smiled, still in a dazed state of orgasm.

Frankie took the soft sponge and covered it in a fresh smelling shower foam, rubbing every part of Cara's body. The feelings were so intense. Frankie had a deep urge to care for Cara, and it was reciprocated both ways.

'This feels so nice.' Cara let out a deep breath as Frankie cleaned her back, enjoying the curve of her body.

'I want to make you feel good,' Frankie said pulling her closer.

'You always do,' Cara replied as she turned around and held on to the moment.

The hot steam filled the bathroom along with the smell of water mint and sea minerals.

They both basked in the air as the hot water fell against their skin.

'I think I love you, Cara,' Frankie whispered.

'I love you, Frankie. I know it.'

17

'I'm getting married,' Mira said with a wide grin on her face.

'You must be joking, mother?' Cara almost spat out her drink.

'No. Me and Phil have decided to take the next step – and before you judge me for my past, he is single.' Mira nodded her head and sipped on her wine. 'Cara, I know I haven't told you before but I am proud of you and I'm happy to see you with someone who makes your eyes light up.'

'Thanks mum. I want you to be happy

too. Do you like Frankie?' Cara tilted her head as she asked.

'I sure do. Look at her out there, making my garden look a million dollars!' Mira nodded towards the window where she had a clear view of Frankie laying down a new planter ready for the summer.

'She is pretty good. We've got the house looking great too.' Cara looked out at Frankie. She loved that woman down to the bare bones. They had been living together pretty much since Frankie opened up to Cara. She just never seemed to leave.

'And how is Jenny doing with her girlfriend?' Mira stood up, pouring another glass of white wine for them both.

'Ah, not so great. Things were going well with Kirsty, but then Jenny got a little drunk and ended up having a fling with Mel – I have no idea why. As you can imagine, Kirsty was devastated, quite rightly so, and Jenny is now in a dilemma. She needs time to figure things out.' Cara rolled her eyes.

'And you said that my life was dramatic. At least married men were straight forward. Lesbians are a fucking nightmare!' Mira laughed.

For the first time in years they were having a normal conversation, enjoying each other's company.

'You're not wrong about that mum, but there are some good ones...'

Cara looked out into the garden and admired Frankie hard at work. Her business had been picking up as the year rolled into the summer months. Cara had been working less at the pub and spending more time building up her own writing business, publishing books online. Doing things that she loved in her life and doing less of what made her unhappy. She had realised what was important to her and what she needed. The happiness she felt with Frankie made her understand that anything was possible.

'Mum, I really love that woman, you know.' Cara felt comfortable enough these days to be open with Mira.

'I can tell. It's in your eyes. The way you look at her says it all – and the way she looks back at you.' Mira smiled.

Life is what you make it.

18

The following weekend Frankie and Cara were sitting out in the back garden on their new decking – which Frankie had done by hand. They sprawled on their loungers, enjoying the early shine of summer.

'This is the life isn't it?' Frankie said with a hearty smile on her face.

'It sure is.' Cara lifted up her glass of Sangria and turned to Frankie.

'I love having more time with you, even though sometimes I still want more.' Frankie turned on her side so she could see Cara better. She had small black shorts on and a white cropped vest. Her body was so tanned from the sun. Her eyes were full of love.

Cara put down her drink and shuffled her chair closer to Frankie. 'More time? I'll just quit work and do jobs with you. Fuck it!' Cara laughed.

'Well maybe one day… but for now we should book a holiday? No work involved just us.' Frankie sat up on the lounger and held Cara's hand. She looked into her piercing blue eyes which always made her feel something in her stomach. She brushed her golden hair behind her ear and traced her hand back down.

'I'd love that.' Cara felt shy and loved.

'Oh, I do have one more thing for you.' Frankie stood up. 'You wait here.'

'If you're going to get the strap on let me know,' Cara said with a smile on her face.

'I'm not actually, just wait there and close your eyes.' Frankie went inside.

A few minutes later a song started playing, Tracy Chapman – Fast Car. Cara's favourite song. A smile took over her face.

Frankie came back outside. 'Keep your eyes shut or there will be real big trouble!'

Cara nodded and kept her eyes squeezed tight.

Frankie slowly knelt down in front of her with the most beautiful, colourful bouquet of flowers and a dark blue box in her hand.

'Okay you can open them now.'

Cara's jaw almost hit the floor as Frankie opened up this small box to display the beautiful topaz ring sat inside.

'Cara, the moment I met you I knew you were something different. I really knew. You are so wonderful, genuine and have the kindest soul. I never ever thought I would want to marry again. I never thought I could love this hard but I love you like nothing else on this earth and beyond. I want you forever and I know we've only been together months but I feel like I've known you a lifetime. I don't want to waste time. Will you marry me?'

Cara's eyes filled with tears. 'Absolutely yes.'

Frankie pushed the ring onto Cara's finger and then wrapped her arms around her, holding her close.

'Jenny is going to call me a stereotypical lesbian. I can't wait!' Cara laughed.

'Life is for living my dear. As long as we are happy that's all that counts. I want you to be my wife. You make me happy every single day.' Frankie took Cara's head in her hands and kissed her gently.

'I am so happy. In fact, sometimes I do question if this isn't really real or if Jenny set this up all along to marry me off and finally be happy,' Cara's said as she scratched her head.

'Mm I knew you were the crazy one

really, not me.' Frankie laughed and got them both a sangria, raising it in the air. 'To us! To living for the moment.'

Cara raised her glass high and looked into the sky with a heart full of joy.

'To love.' She shouted before jumping in the air with excitement. 'I need to tell Jenny!' Cara got out her phone and rang Jenny, putting her on speakerphone.

'Hello, are you okay?' Jenny said in a sleepy voice.

'I've got news. We're engaged!' Cara's excitement bursting through her words.

'Oh my god, you crazy pair! I'm happy for you. Congrats! You're such *stereotypical lesbians.*' Jenny said, making Cara look at Frankie and raise her eyebrows.

'Thank you! I know, and we love every second of it. Where are you?' Cara knew she was upto something.

'I'm in... bed.' Jenny wasn't giving much away with her tone of voice either.

'Who with?'

'Erhm, Mel... and Kirsty,' Jenny sheepishly admitted.

'You filthy cow. I LOVE it.' Cara and Frankie broke into laughter.

'They both say hello.' Jenny began to laugh too.

'Well I won't hold you up, get back to your scrum,' Cara said as she tried to hold some laughter back.

'Love you, bye.' Jenny ended the call.

Frankie picked up Cara and wrapped her legs around her sides.

They laughed in the sunshine enjoying the moment and simplicity of each other.

Although they had two contrasting pasts, what defined them now was nothing more than the foundations of true love and a great belief that life is for living. Frankie knew that all too well and Cara was happy to give it everything she had.

THANKS FOR READING!

Grace Parkes

Hey, thank you so much for reading my book. I really do hope that you enjoyed it! I would be grateful if you could spare a moment to leave a review on Amazon – they really do make a difference for Indie authors like myself.

MAILING LIST

Please sign up to my mailing to be the first to know about my new releases! You'll also receive monthly free stuff as a little thank you:
https://mailchi.mp/
2a09276da35f/graceparkeswrites

SOCIAL MEDIA

If you'd like to get in touch or twitter.com/GraceParkesFic keep up to date with what I'm up to, here's where to find me!

Twitter: https://www.twitter.com/GraceParkesFic

Facebook: https://www.facebook.com/graceparkesauthor

Email: graceparkeswrites@hotmail.com

Please check out my other books. They are all available to read for free on Kindle Unlimited.

PLEASE MISTRESS

Fiona can't wait to leave her dysfunctional family life, her safe boyfriend and the small town she grew up in far behind her when she goes to Music School in the city.

She needs to figure out what she wants in life and love, but there seem to be more questions than answers.

Then there is her growing obsession with her aloof singing teacher, Joss Red.

Will Fiona find a way to tell Joss about her fantasies?

Find out here: getbook.at/pleasemistress

BITTERSWEET SHE

Tasha Robinson thought her average life would never change. For years Tasha had continued to stay in the same job, town and stale relationship – none of which brought excitement into her life.

As societal pressures smother Tasha, a weekend away with her best friend changes everything, but has it changed for the better? Tasha meets a captivating girl who takes her breath away and is forced to make some difficult decisions which could potentially change her life forever.

A fun and intense romance from exciting new lesfic author Grace Parkes.

Get it here: getbook.at/BittersweetShe

GUITAR GIRL

GUITAR GIRL

Guitar Girl Ava Sierra knew from a young age that she was destined for the stage. What she didn't know was the turbulent drama that was on its way into her life.

As she battles it out for the chance to break through into the music industry with her rebellious band, she collides with rival Charlotte Thunder who seems all too familiar.

Loud music, unrequited love and an

unexpected chain of events will keep you turning pages in this new exciting lesfic by budding author Grace Parkes.

Get it here: getbook.at/GuitarGirl

HER SECRET

HER SECRET

Her Secret Sarah and Emily had everything they ever wanted, except a happy relationship.
After new girl Megan Jenkinson started working alongside Sarah, life began to change.

They embark on a heated affair which takes them both by surprise, especially Megan who had always been into guys.

Lies and deceit take everyone on a gripping adventure throughout this new steamy lesfic by exciting author Grace Parkes.

Disclaimer - this book contains cheating please don't read if you do not like this topic

UNTITLED

Get it here: mybook.to/hersecretlesfic

Printed in Dunstable, United Kingdom